A TEMPLAR BOOK

First published in hardback and softback in the UK in 2015 by Templar Publishing,
an imprint of The Templar Company Limited,
Deepdene Lodge, Deepdene Avenue, Dorking, Surrey, RH5 4AT

First edition

ISBN 978-1-78370-082-0 (hardback)
ISBN 978-1-78370-083-7 (softback)

Printed in China

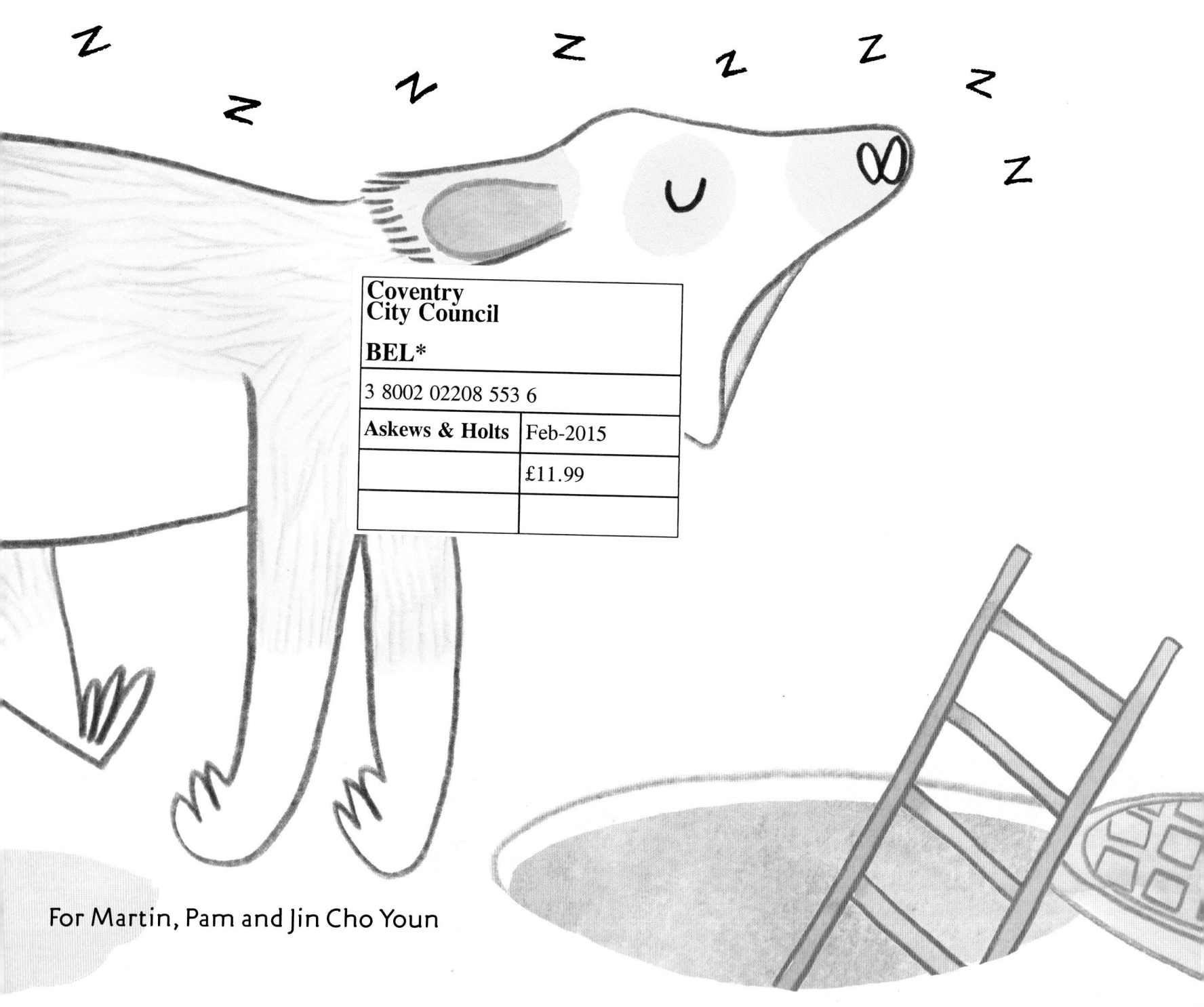

For Martin, Pam and Jin Cho Youn

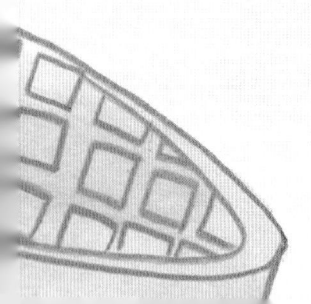

– I can't watch!

LEMUR DREAMER

Courtney Dicmas

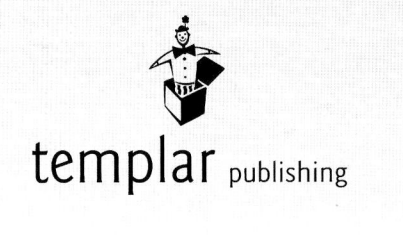

templar publishing

The residents of 32 Pebbly Lane
led mostly unextraordinary lives.

All except one, that is.

Louis, who lived on the very top floor,

had the unfortunate habit...

of **sleepwalking!**

Every night, fast asleep, Louis wandered out his front door, snoozed around the other apartments, and snuffled back to bed.

It wasn't a problem at first.

The neighbours were very understanding.

But as time went on,

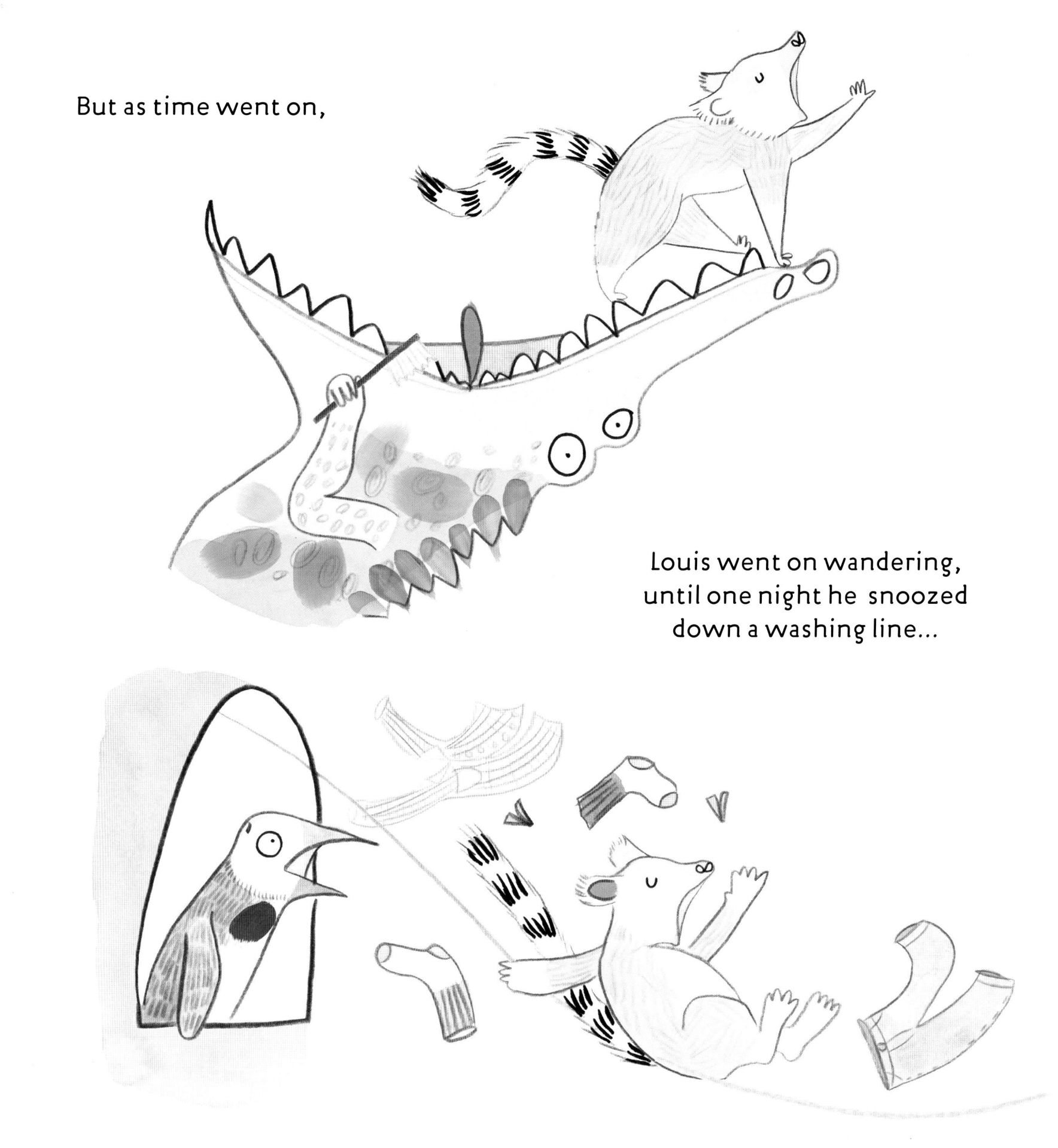

Louis went on wandering,
until one night he snoozed
down a washing line...

and snuffled
right out onto
Pebbly Lane!

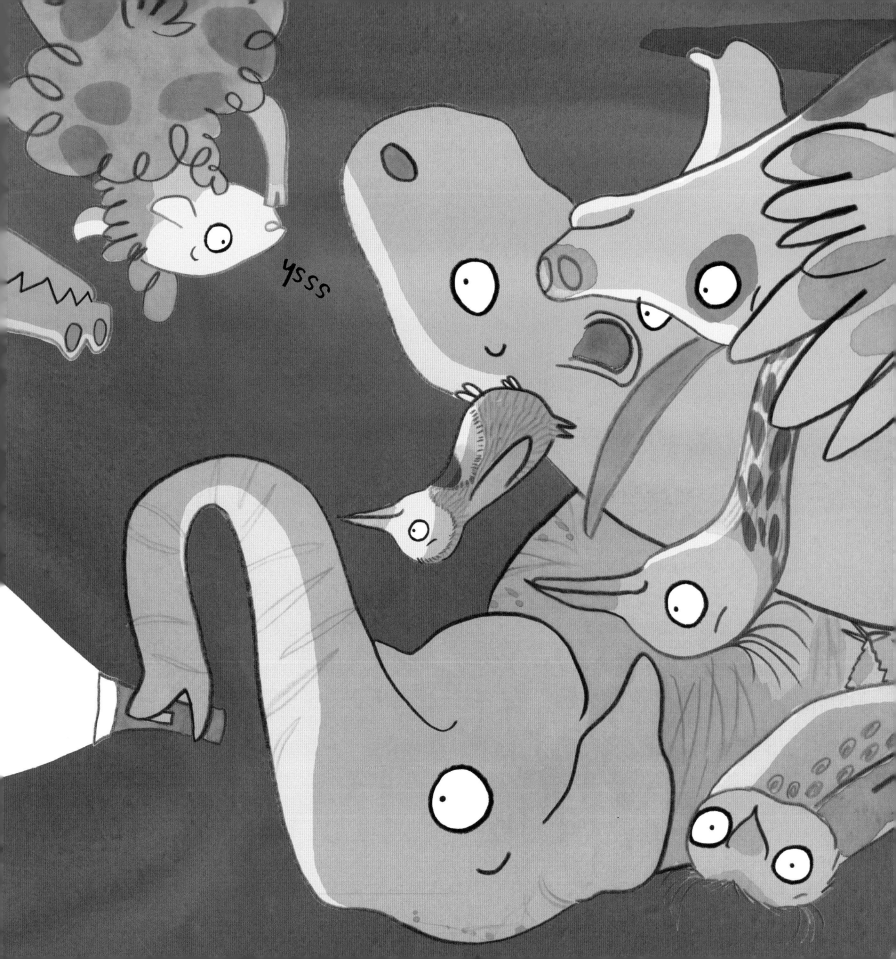

This was getting out of hand.
"Where's Louis going?" whispered his friends.
"What shall we do?"

"There's just one thing for it," said Little Bird.
"We will have to walk with him."

So as Louis snored beyond
Pebbly Lane, his friends
tip-toed close behind.

No one knew what he was dreaming of.

But whatever it was...

and wherever he went...

his friends followed fearlessly.

Until, at last...

Louis ran out of places to sleepwalk.

"WAKE UP, LOUIS!!!"

shouted his friends.

But Louis was still fast asleep.
Could they reach him in time?

OOOF!

Safely back on the cliff,
lucky Louis sat up,
blinked twice
and YAWNED.

"I had the MOST amazing dreams
last night," he said.

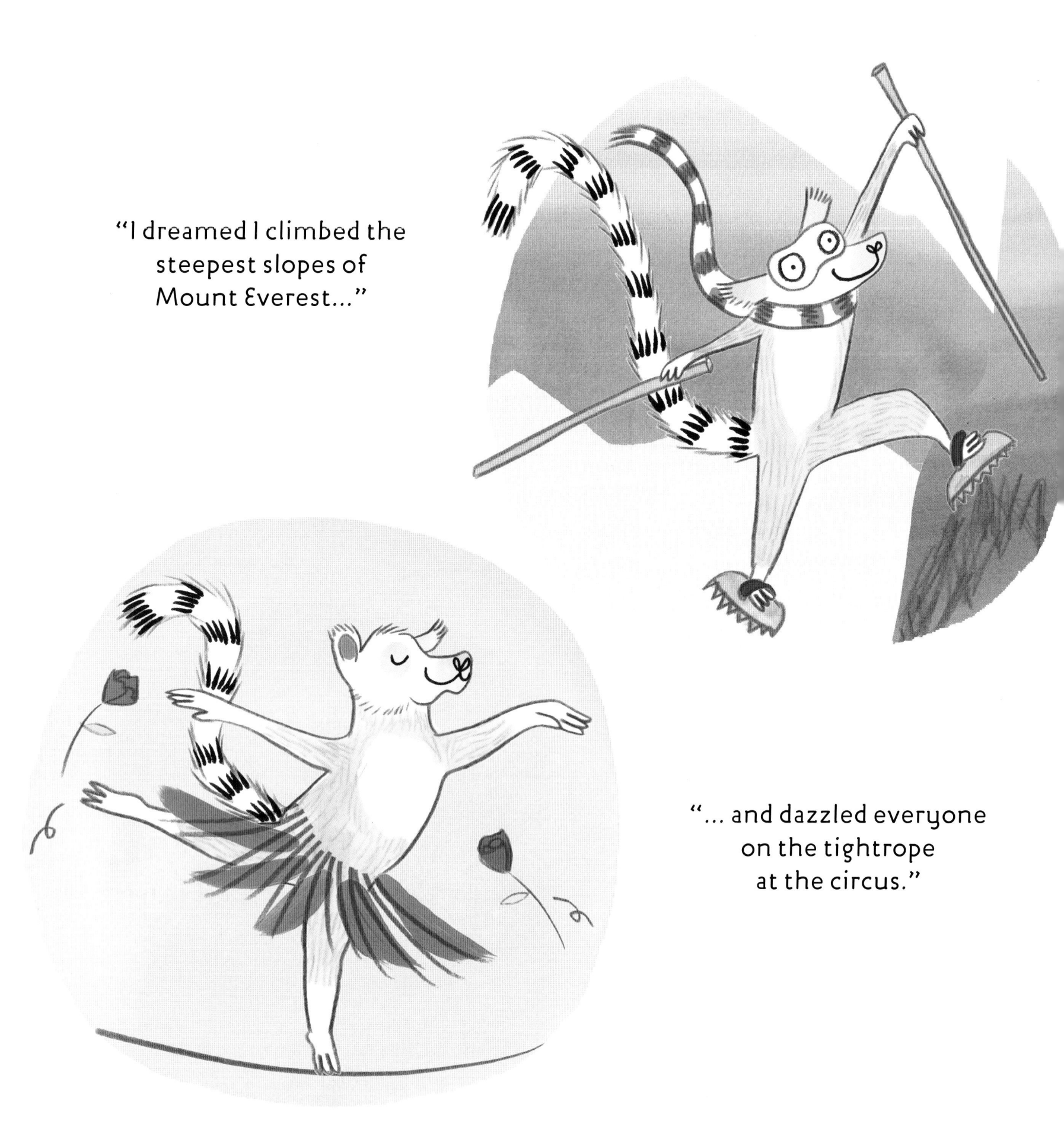

"I dreamed I climbed the steepest slopes of Mount Everest..."

"... and dazzled everyone on the tightrope at the circus."

"Then, I was just about to go scuba diving on the Great Barrier Reef, when something stopped me."

"But where am I? And what are you all doing here?

Hang on a minute..."

"I've been sleepwalking again!"

Louis felt terrible. He'd caused his friends so much trouble.
But they didn't mind. They loved Louis, even with all his snoozing and snuffling.

So to cheer him up, the next day his friends decided to get Louis a special present.

Something
that would keep him safe,
no matter where his
dreams took him.

Because that's what friends are for.